Dear Pig Fans,

Pigs in the Corner: Fun with Math and Dance is the eighth title in the Pigs Will Be Pigs math series. It's all about SPATIAL SENSE and DIRECTION! When I was in elementary school, those words frightened me, as did just about everything that had to do with math. I never realized that math was all around us in our daily lives. That's why I wrote the Pigs Will Be Pigs books, which (by the way) are all based on true family adventures. I used to love to go to my children's school and watch them square dance in gym class. I noticed that sometimes students missed the directions and mixed up right and left. That's when I had a great idea: Having the Pigs square dance would be a fun way to learn all about spatial sense and direction. So follow these easy steps:

1) Read **Pigs in the Corner** just for fun!

2) Go back and read the story again. Look at the pages of Mr. Pig's square dancing manual. In which direction do the gals move when pairing off with the gents? In which direction do the gents move when pairing off with the gals?

3) How many dances do you know? Think of the ways in which math is involved.

4) Answer the math questions at the end of the book. You can do this by yourself, with your parents, or with your teacher.

Remember the Pig Family Motto:

MATH + READING = FUN

Love,
Amy Axelrod

P.S. For Parents and Teachers Only
The Pigs Will Be Pigs books have been designed around the National Council of Teachers of Mathematics's Thirteen Standards. Use them as picture book read-alouds initially, and then as vehicles to introduce, reinforce, and review the concepts and skills particular to each title.

Pigs  in the Corner

Fun with Math and Dance

story by **Amy Axelrod**

pictures by **Sharon McGinley-Nally**

Simon & Schuster Books for Young Readers

New York   London   Toronto   Sydney   Singapore

Mrs. Pig and the piglets were waiting on pins and needles.

"What's wrong?" asked Mrs. Pig.

"It seems our dancing teacher has come down with a cold and lost his voice," said Mr. Pig.

"What a shame," said Mrs. Pig. "Now the recital will have to be cancelled."

"Oh, no!" cried the piglets as they stepped to their right and passed each other back-to-back. "Grandma and Grandpa said they couldn't wait to see us do-si-do."

"No problem," said Mr. Pig. "I volunteered to take over. The show must go on."

"Great idea," said Mrs. Pig, "except for one thing."

"What's that?" asked Mr. Pig.

"You've never called a square dance before."

"Easy as pie," said Mr. Pig. "We've been practicing for weeks. I know the steps by heart. You'll see, I'll bring down the house."

"Well then, pardners," said Mrs. Pig, . . .

Let's  face

the music!

The Pigs swung by Grandma and Grandpa's and then headed straight for the recital hall.

"Mom, if Dad's the new caller, then who's gonna dance with you?" asked the piglets.

"Oops, I hadn't thought of that," said Mrs. Pig. "I guess I'll have to sit the dance out."

"Says who! You know, Grandpa used to be quite a hoofer in his day," said Grandma.

"That's right," said Grandpa. "I still remember a thing or two. I'd be delighted to fill in."

Everyone was waiting for the Pigs.

"Yahoo!" shouted the piglets.

Grandma moved halfway up the bleachers and took a seat smack in the center. *I should get an eyeful up here,* she thought.

Meanwhile, Mrs. Pig did a quick run-through with Grandpa, while Mr. Pig reviewed the square dancing manual.

RULES

for a Square Dancing Caller

1. *Be neat and friendly. Always look good in your best square dancing clothes. Remember to wear a big smile.*

2. *Be an expert. Know your square dancing calls by heart. Never go too fast or too slow.*

3. *Be creative. Don't be afraid to make up new calls, as long as your dancers can keep up with you.*

4. *Be professional. Never bother musicians while they are playing.*

5. *Be safe. Never have your dancers swing too wildly. Square dancing is fun.*

Mr. Pig joined the musicians onstage.

The dancers squared off into sets of couples. The gals moved to the right, and the gents moved to the left.

"Testing, testing, one two three," said Mr. Pig as he tapped the microphone.

"Now, gals and gents in this dancin' hall,
I'm Mr. Pig; I'll make the calls.
Shout a howdy, stomp that floor,
Bow and curtsy to that pal of yours.

"Gals be polite, once again,
Curtsy now to your corner friend.
Gents bow to your ladies, corners all,
Bow to your mother across the hall.

"Now, here comes my favorite part,
So do it right, from the start.
Swing that lady then do-si-do,
Swing her high, swing her low.

"Now promenade her out in the hall,
Promenade her till next fall.
Promenade him all through town,
Promenade in that dancin' gown.

"NOW SWING! EVERYBODY SWING!"
Oh, no, panicked Mr. Pig. *If I can't see the dancers, I'll never remember the calls. I'm in big trouble.*

I'll just have to wing it, thought Mr. Pig as he took a deep breath.

"All sets join, with a wickety whack,
Circle the hall then circle back.
Slide to the left, count to ten,
Slide to the right, then do it again.

"Now back to your sets, don't be late,
Be quick, before I count to eight.
And six steps backward, gents and gals,
Turn around and make new pals.

"Swing your darlin'. Swing your honey.
Swing her fast, with a face that's funny."

Mr. Pig carried on.

"Sidestep to four, then say 'good-bye.'
Toss your gal,
Straight up to the sky.

"All join center lick-a-dee scoot.
Hop eight times, on your dancin' foot.
Then switch over to the other one,
Eight more times and now you're done.

"Now gals and gents in this dancin' hall,
I'm Mr. Pig; I made the calls.
Hope you liked what I had to say,
I guess that's it, so have a fine day!

"Dear," said Mr. Pig to Mrs. Pig, "I'll bet you're really proud of me. I told you I'd bring down the . . ."

A Beginner's Square Dancing Dictionary

circle—All four couples in the set join hands to form a circle, and move either to the right or to the left.

corner—A gal's corner is the gent to her right. A gent's corner is the gal to his left.

couple—A gal and her gent. Or, a gent and his gal. In a square dancing set there are four couples. A gal always stands to the right of her gent. Or, a gent always stands to the left of his gal.

do-si-do—A gent and a gal face each other and pass at the right shoulder. Then they sidestep to the right and after passing back to back, they return home.

home—Where a gal and her gent stand on the square.

honor—When a gent bows to his own gal, or to his corner gal. And when a gal holds her skirt and curtsies to her own gent or to her corner gent.

promenade—When a gent stands to the left of a gal and reaches over her right shoulder to hold her right hand while they clasp left hands together in front of themselves.

set—The square where the four dancing couples stand, all facing the center of the square. The first couple stands with their backs to the caller. The second couple is to the right of couple one. The third couple is to the right of couple two and the fourth couple is to the right of couple three. Couples one and three are called the head couples. Couples two and four are the side couples.

swing—A gal and her gent link elbows and, keeping the balls of their right feet on the ground, they swing around each other by pushing with their left feet.

COUPLE 3

COUPLE 2

COUPLE 4

COUPLE 1
**(They always stand
with their backs to the caller.)**

1. Which side couple stands to the right of the first couple?
2. Which couple stands opposite of the first couple?
3. Which couple stands to the left of the fourth couple?

**Bonus: How many rules did Mr. Pig break while calling the square dance?
Do you think it would be possible to square dance to Mr. Pig's calls?**

For Annika Elizabeth McGinley,
and special thanks to Amy Axelrod and Anahid Hamparian
–S. M·N.

For my David,
and thanks to
Sharon McGinley-Nally,
my pig pardner,
and to my good friend
Anahid Hamparian,
and many thanks also to
Mrs. Pat Tosi, who taught my boys
how to square dance
–A. A.

SIMON & SCHUSTER BOOKS FOR YOUNG READERS
An imprint of Simon & Schuster Children's Publishing Division
1230 Avenue of the Americas, New York, New York 10020

Text copyright © 2001 by Amy Axelrod
Illustrations copyright © 2001 by Sharon McGinley-Nally

SIMON & SCHUSTER BOOKS FOR YOUNG READERS is a trademark of Simon & Schuster.

Book design by Anahid Hamparian
The text for this book is set in 17-point Baskerville.
The illustrations are rendered in ink, watercolor, and acrylic.

Printed in Hong Kong
2 4 6 8 10 9 7 5 3 1

Library of Congress Cataloging-in-Publication Data
Axelrod, Amy.
Pigs in the corner : fun with math and dance /
story by Amy Axelrod ;
pictures by Sharon McGinley-Nally.—1st ed.
p. cm.–(Pigs will be pigs)
Summary: Mr. Pig fills in for the missing caller at the square dancing recital
ISBN 0-689-82470-X
[1. Square dancing–Fiction. 2. Left and right–Fiction. 3. Pigs–Fiction.]
I. McGinley-Nally, Sharon, ill. II. Title.
PZ7.A96155 Pe 2001
[Fic]–dc21
00-063532

first·
edition